For all the families, big and small,
who muddled through 2020.
Always look for rainbows.

D1421984

ISBN: 978-1-913339-19-7
Published by Owlet Press Ltd, November 2020
Text copyright - Lauren Fennemore 2020
Illustrations copyright - Zoe Damoulakis 2020

THE YEAR WE MUDDLED THROUGH

Written by Lauren Fennemore

Illustrated by Zoe Damoulakis

First published in the UK
by Owlet Press
www.owletpress.com

Someday when you're much older
and much bigger than right now,
you might just ask about the year
the world turned upside down.

When lots was lost — but some things found —
in struggles steep uphill,
when schools and shops and businesses
all quietly stood still.

And one day when you're older, I might tell you how life changed,
how we learnt new ways to do things in a world so rearranged.
But while you're still so little, here's what I think I'll do —
I'll tell you all the good things from the year we muddled through ...

Our road became quite empty, free from all the usual traffic,
the buses, cars and motorbikes just disappeared like magic!

It had never been so quiet, things had never been so still,
and when darkness came and sleep arrived,
all was calm ... until ...

... a family of foxes darted swiftly from a hedge,

an owl swooped from the treetops
and perched on a window's edge,

... the nearby flock of fluffy sheep
escaped the farmer's pen

and were followed
by four pigs,
three cows,
two llamas
and one hen.

Lit only by the smiling moon,
our road came back to life,
without the usual noisiness,
the animals ran rife!

They danced across the garden fence
and munched on all the green.

They even clambered on the roof
of number seventeen!

And only on occasion was their night ever disturbed,
but no human dared admit that they'd seen something so absurd.

So their parties stayed a secret, no one knew about their fun,
and the animals all scarpered home with every rising sun.

When morning broke and curtains drew,
not one of us suspected,
the animal shenanigans
that happened undetected.

Too wrapped up in our thoughts of
what the day before had taught us,
too wishful and distracted
by the hope a new one brought us.

And each new dawn would somehow
make the previous seem duller,
as endless sparkling rainbows
filled the sky with vibrant colour.

On daily walks we always
counted every one we saw,
and it took less than five minutes
to reach one hundred and four!

Each building and each office block, each home and hotel suite,
had rainbows bursting from their windows, right down to the street.
Bright bridges over rooftops formed when rainbows would collide,

and from every child's bedroom —
a multicoloured slide!

Despite what people told us, we searched but never found,
a single pot of gold where any rainbow hit the ground.
Instead we'd find a different kind of pot containing treasure—
the tallest ever sunflowers, too high for us to measure!

One grew above the houses, passed the rainbows, through the cloud,
with giant leafy branches that could shelter any crowd.
And people started thinking: "Should we climb up to the top?"
"Should we find a way to slow it down or try to make it stop?"

But someone else — a man named Jack — recounted an old tale,
of magic beans and giants and a boy who did prevail.
He told us how, just once before, he'd seen a plant so tall,
and we would all fare better letting nature make the call.

So we sat and watched it growing, getting bigger every day,
until the yellow petals grew to reach the Milky Way!

And without the usual aeroplanes filling the night sky,
as well as stars and planets, now a flower caught our eye.

And these visions made us wonder, whilst normality was tested,
perhaps our precious planet Earth felt finally quite rested?

With skies and plants and animals all thriving from the break,
we saw first-hand how life could look in 2020's wake.

We started seeing everything
with new appreciation,

so grateful for the things we had,
we clapped across the nation.

In spite of all the changes, the Earth continued turning,
and inside our little household, something special was occurring.

With every day and every week
and every month that passed,
someone quite miraculous
was growing oh—so fast!

In a world we weren't quite used to,
at a time so full of fear,
whilst everything felt muddled,
I'll still look back on that year ...

... and remember dancing animals and stars that filled the sky,
with rainbows on each corner and sunflowers so high.

And one day when you ask about
the year we muddled through,
I'll remember love and strength and hope.

All of it for YOU!